Reluctant Bride

and other Short Stories from Papua New Guinea

JORDAN DEAN

First Edition: December, 2017

The moral right of the author has been asserted.

Published by JDT Publications
Port Moresby, National Capital District, Papua New Guinea
Email: jdtpublications@gmail.com

National Library of Papua New Guinea
Cataloguing-in-Publication entry:

Dean, Jordan. 1984 — .
    Reluctant Bride & other Short Stories from Papua New Guinea.

    ISBN-13: 978-9980-89-986-6

    1. Short Stories, Papua New Guinea. 1. Fiction
PNG/823-dc 22

Printed in USA by CreateSpace Independent Publishing.

This one is for my family for believing in me.
And to my readers, hope you enjoy the stories in this collection.

I would like to thank Ed Brumby and Chips Mackellar for the comments, suggestions and editorial assistance. You both are the best editors I've come across. Thank you.

CONTENTS

JORDAN DEAN

RELUCTANT BRIDE

Angela Mono was a smart young lawyer from Southern Highlands. After completing her law degree, she continued her studies at the Legal Training Institute and was admitted to the bar. After graduation she had no trouble finding employment with Warner Shand Lawyers, a reputable international law firm. She had everything one would define as 'successful' by Papua New Guinean standards; a good remuneration package, a car and a decent three bedroom house. As far as she was concerned, life was great. She had been dating Peter Wanpis, a Western Highlands man for over a year but she wasn't in a rush to get married and have kids.

That Saturday morning, her mum decided to drop by unexpectedly, along with another woman and her uncle. Angela thought it was one of her mother's girlfriend paying a casual visit.

"Hi mum. You didn't inform me that you were coming over with a friend. Can I get you anything?" she offered, happy to see them. "Water? Apple or orange juice?"

"We are fine. We dropped by to talk to you about something important," her mum said.

"Oh? What is it then?" Angela sat down next to her mum.

"I talked to your father and he agrees with me that Peter is a good choice for you. You're not getting any younger, you know. All your cousins have two to three kids already and have all settled down. That's what you should be thinking about."

Angela didn't say anything. She was taken aback by what her mother just said. When the other woman was introduced as Peter's mum she had a bad feeling in the pit of her stomach.

"Angela, we understand you've been doing great in your career and we are all very proud of you. But my daughter, it is time for you to settle down. We just want you to be happy. We are looking out for your best interest," her uncle said.

As a Papua New Guinean, Angela realized that her family had expectations of her that she hated but felt the need to fulfil them. At twenty eight, she was considered old and late in the bearing of children. The fact that she still hadn't settled down with a husband seemed to be the biggest crime to her family.

"I am twenty eight, going on twenty nine," she finally spoke from her shock and utter nightmare.

"Angela, I talked to my son. He speaks highly of you and obviously approves of you," Peter's mum began.

"Approves of me?" Angela stared at her in dismay.

"Not just him, but so do I. We will arrange for your bride price and I would of course take you as my daughter and welcome you to Peter's family."

Peter's mum smiled encouragingly. She was a nice woman, small in stature compared to Peter. Angela took a deep breath, calming herself.

No! She thought for a while. This isn't happening! I am not going to let mum take control of my life as though I was a child.

"I am not marrying Peter," she said boldly, looking at each of them in the eye. "Thank you for coming all the way over here but it's not going to work out between me and Peter."

"You two have been going out for over a year," her mother stated, as though dating meant marriage.

"Yes, we have. But, I am not ready for marriage mum. I am sorry Mrs. Wanpis and Uncle Paul for having to come all the way over here."

"Angela!" her mother snapped but managed to smile at Peter's mother although embarrassed. "She doesn't know what she is saying."

"Yes mum, actually, I completely understand what I am saying and my answer is no! I will not marry Peter. Peter and I are not suited for each other. I am sure there are women out there for him, but it's definitely not me."

Angela leaned back feeling calmer than ever. Looking at her mother, she saw herself in twenty years' time. Her mom was a striking woman with her dark brown skin. She had extension hair, light make-up and wore a *meri blouse*. To Angela, her mum had always been the epitome of a highlands woman. She believed in culture and customs, contributed to so many bride price ceremonies, funerals and compensations but ruled with an iron fist. Though she had asked Angela to follow the ways of their people, she herself had refused to remarry.

Angela firmly believed in the freedom of not having to answer to anyone. She knew her mum's marriage had not worked out due to her father marrying a second wife which her mum didn't like.

Angela was annoyed at them and she wasn't going to let them make choices for her that she did not agree with. She was a twenty eight year old educated women, liberated and independent. She was going to act like she did not just have a brain in her head to think for herself but she also had a damn backbone.

"Uncle, auntie and mum, I am not trying to be rude or disrespectful but I have things to do. Please feel free to stay as long as you want but I have a life to live."

Angela left her mother with a gaping mouth along with the other two who were equally shocked. She made her way out to her car and drove straight to Peter's house. He smiled at her as though nothing had happened, which pissed her even more.

"We are done!" she told him straight to his face. "No man, not even my father would force me to marry, nor will I let any man control me."

"What are you talking about?" he asked, surprised at her outburst.

"I am not a child, Peter, and I am not cheap either."

"Cheap? I never said that."

"No, but I am not some village lady that you can make arrangements to marry!"

Peter rubbed his forehead, looking confused. "I wasn't aware of any arrangements Angela."

"I am done. Thanks for everything, but I can't do this shit anymore. Your mum's at my house right now."

She walked off towards her car.

"Angela please?"

"Oh, you heard me. Get over yourself," she smirked from the pathway.

For some strange reason that she could not understand, her life seemed to be turning upside down. She picked up her cell phone and dialed her friend Tasha's number.

"Hi, what's up Angie?" Tasha answered after what seemed like the fifth ring.

"Tash, I need a few shots of tequila and someone to talk to. Can we catch up please?"

"Oh? You having a bad day?"

Angela sighed. "I just can't believe we still have arranged marriages! Anyway, I'll bore you with the details later."

LADY IN THE BLACK DRESS

I saw them while I was pouring a drink for a customer.

The lady, probably in her early twenties, wore the hottest black dress I had ever seen. She had soft features and curly hair. The man, an elderly expatriate, had a balding head with the little hair remaining being grey.

It was becoming a norm to see very young Papua New Guinean ladies my age hanging out with expatriate men who were probably their grandfather's age. I guessed it's about the money this days.

The man sat up to reveal an annoyed look on his face. His lips kept moving, but with the noise of people singing a happy birthday song in a nearby table, I couldn't hear what he was saying to her. It seemed clear that they were arguing about something.

I braced myself, and put on a genuine smile on my face to welcome them.

"Hi. What would you like to drink, Sir? Ma'am?" I asked politely.

They both declined to drink. So, I went to serve other customers, all the while glancing back at them. At one time, the lady waved at me and asked for a glass of cold water.

"Here you go ma'am."

She took the glass gently and started sipping the cold water. She then lowered her head and kept quiet.

Another customer called for me. As I poured his drink, I heard the expatriate man hissing harsh words. The young lady looked miserable with pleading eyes. After muttering something under his breath, the man turned to the lady, yanked her by her arm and headed to the door.

"Ma'am?" I called after them.

The man turned around, seething. The lady did not even acknowledge the fact that I was addressing her.

"You forgot your purse." I stretched my hand out, holding the small purse.

In a split second he snatched it from my hand and practically ran to the door with the lady trailing behind him.

The rest of the week was hectic. I didn't really like the job very much, but I held on to it as a decent source of income. While I had been a student at the University of Papua New Guinea, I worked part time as a bartender at the Gold Club during semester breaks. I needed the money to pay for my tuition fees. Dad was unemployed and mum's salary was not enough to make ends meet. As the eldest girl in the family, I felt it was my responsibility to support the family financially.

My job made me witness bizarre stuff happening from time to time. But, I never forgot about that incident. I kept wondering during the rest of the week about the fate of the abused young lady.

One week later, I entered the club from the back door, and got ready for my shift. A mental preparation was essential for me in order to face all different types of characters out there at the bar.

People came with different issues. Some had marital issues. Others hung out to celebrate an awesome week or to forget a depressing one. Sometimes, I would listen to their nonsense. Other times, I simply ignored them when they started hitting on me. I tried to keep my distance as much as possible.

I saw her again as I came out to the counter. She was sitting rigidly in the same seat as before. Her eyes were staring at the glass between her hands. Since she never raised her head, I took the opportunity to look at her for a few seconds. She looked as elegant as before.

I started serving the other customers, all the time aware of her and her calm state. I thought about asking her what was going on, or, considering what had happened last time, if she needed help. It was weird how she had that effect on me. Then I remembered the club's rules to never interfere with a client's affairs.

In the midst of all of these thoughts crowding my head, and pouring drinks, I heard her soft voice.

"How much do you want?"

For a second, I thought she was talking to me. I turned around and realized that she was talking to a man sitting next to her in close proximity. He looked her age. He wore a faded jean and t-shirt that definitely made him look out of place.

As I was cleaning the glasses, I studied him. He was tall, had curly hair and tattoos on his arm. My best guess was that they were both from Central.

"I need some money for…" His voice trailed off when he noticed that I had been watching.

I quickly turned my eyes away, and pretended that a customer had called me from the other side of the counter. After making sure that he wasn't looking, I started wiping the counter. I kept stealing side glances when I had the chance. There was something about the lady that fascinated me.

She opened her purse, counted some notes and gave it to the young man. The two looked intimate.

"Thank you." He smiled.

He raised his glass and gulped the whole drink in one motion. Later, he cleared his throat, and called for me.

"Another round please."

A few seconds later and his drink was ready. At that moment, she looked up and our eyes met. I saw a look of recognition on her face. She quickly lowered her head, pretending that nothing was out of the ordinary. She pretended that she had never seen me before.

The night went by fast and awkward for me. It was the first time I felt uncomfortable in my job. I had the feeling that I wasn't supposed to know she was there with someone else. It bothered my conscious and I sighed inwardly, praying for my shift to end as soon as possible.

"Excuse me?"

I turned and was surprised when I realized it was the lady. She was asking me for something. What could she possibly want? The young man was no longer there.

"Yes, ma'am?" I said hesitantly.

"You didn't see me tonight."

I cleared my throat. "I'm sorry?"

"I said, you didn't see me tonight."

"I don't know what you're talking about, ma'am."

"Good," she said, finishing her drink.

With that, she left as if she hadn't talked to me. I stared at her until she walked out. She seemed so certain that I had remembered her and the fiasco that happened two weeks ago. What baffled me was that she was also certain that I wouldn't tell. But, tell who? I thought.

Two days later, I saw the expatriate man again. He was standing at the counter gripping the edges, clearly impatient. I noticed that he was fuming and his eyes darkened as I headed his way holding a towel.

"Hey you!" He recognized me and pointed.

I stopped in my tracks and just stared blankly at him. There was something intimidating about him. I decided to act as if I hadn't seen him before.

"Hello Sir, what can I get you?"

"I'm not here to drink."

"Okay," I said slowly, putting the towel away.

He took a deep breath. "Have you seen her?"

Now, that's a surprise. I never thought he'd ask me that.

I tried to stall him a bit, not really knowing what to do. Actually, I was not sure what was going to happen if I didn't tell him what he wanted to know. It was not going to be good either way. He looked at me with sincerity this time.

"Please…"

His facial expression changed so quickly from anger to helpless and defeated. I didn't answer him, still trying to figure out what to do.

He let out a long sigh. "Please. I have to get to the bottom of this. Did you or did you not see my wife here with someone yesterday?"

I didn't realize that I was so nervous. I felt myself torn asunder here. Should I answer him, be honest and straightforward like the kind of person I am? Or should I just lie in order to save the lady from the wrath of a jealous husband? But whom should I trust here? Two weeks ago, she seemed like a victim to me. But after last night…

"Hey! I asked you a question. The least you could do is answer me," he said.

My thoughts trailed off when I realized that he was still talking to me. I stood there motionless, not knowing what to do. I had to decide, to act, to give an answer. But, for the life of me, I didn't know what to say.

I put on a fake smile. "Would you like a drink, Sir?"

TEN MISSED CALLS

I stared at the notifications on my phone screen. Putting down my cup of coffee, I picked up the phone, debating whether to call Amanda or not.

I had ignored all ten calls and every text message Amanda had sent me over the past week. I just didn't know how to reply to her anymore.

"Jay, pick up the phone. We need to talk about this."

That was the last text message she sent me, five days ago. When she first told me the news, I was shocked. We took every precaution. I got so pissed I overreacted. I wasn't ready for a baby and I knew my mum would go berserk if I told her.

Amanda was the mature one in our relationship. She tried to calm me, promised me it would be okay and that we would figure it out. But at twenty two, I was so focused on enjoying my life and climbing up the corporate hierarchy. I walked away and ignored her calls thereafter.

"Jay?"

A soft voice made me look up. A woman, who reminded me so much of Amanda at first glance, stood in front of my desk. She smiled politely.

Marion, the receptionist was a friendly and very pretty young woman who dropped by my desk occasionally to chat.

"Yes Marion, what can I do for you?" I responded, trying to remain professional.

"Are you okay?" she asked, studying me.

Marion had no idea how much of an impact her question had. A pain grew in my chest. I felt like a total failure. I was running away from my own child. I tried to detach myself from my emotions but it was simply not possible.

"Not too good," I said quietly.

The guilt on my face must have given away the fact there was more to it.

"Take it easy Jay," she said and returned to her table.

I had to complete my reports or face the wrath of my bosses. There were three emails in my inbox. Two were spam messages. God knows why the company paid so much money for a spam filter! The other email was about a new contract to provide taxation services for a catering company.

I tried to work on my reports but couldn't concentrate. My conscience tormented me and it was beginning to wear me down.

After work, I caught a thirty minute ride by cab to Amanda's apartment. As I approached her apartment gate, I began to consider what to say. I was afraid of facing my own pregnant girlfriend.

What if she wasn't home? What if she didn't want to see me?

I kept walking and before my thoughts got too out of control, I was in front of her door. I took a deep breath, anxious for what was to come. There was no turning back now.

I knocked on the door and waited patiently. Everything felt so obscure and pretty messed up. My legs trembled.

Grow some balls and don't run!

I almost didn't notice Amanda as the door opened and she appeared in front of me.

"Jay?"

It sounded as though she was both surprised and questioning why I was there. I took in a deep breath. My gaze drifted from her eyes to her abdomen. It wasn't bulging but looking at it made my own stomach twist.

"Hi Amanda." I swallowed hard and ran a hand through my hair. Another nervous moment.

Amanda would have smiled at my awkwardness, but the situation that brought us together prevented it. Instead, she stepped aside and welcomed me into her apartment.

As I took a seat and waited for her to sit next to me, I organized my thoughts. She positioned herself on the other end of the couch. I could tell she too was very deep in thought.

"I want the child and I want to be with you," I said, breaking the silence.

Amanda bit her lip, looking down at the floor. I guessed she was considering not taking me back. She could manage on her own and didn't need me. I didn't blame her. She must have spent the last week full of anxiety, trying to plan what her future would be like. Despite her hesitation, I was prepared to support her now, regardless of how long it took for her to forgive me.

"I had an abortion," she announced before I could go on further.

I was dumbfounded. My thoughts burnt like fire, spreading to my chest and stomach and I suddenly felt nauseated. I must have heard wrong.

"What?" I had to ask.

Amanda shifted closer to me. She put her hand on my knee and spoke softly. "I just... I just couldn't do it alone."

The words struck me like another explosion in my core. I didn't deserve this woman. The one who comforted me while I sat there speechless. I looked into her deep brown eyes and saw my own reflection. A scared, irresponsible man.

"I'm sorry." I lowered my head in remorse and shame.

Tears built up in Amanda's eyes. She put her face in her hands and trembled as her emotions took over. I wondered how many times she broke down while I had avoided her calls.

I couldn't take it any longer. I took her into my arms and pulled her onto my lap. As I embraced her, she leaned her head on my chest. I knew I had let her down.

"I am sorry," I murmured again, not knowing what else to say.

Eventually, our differences outweighed the positives in our relationship and we had to call it quits. I'm grateful that she had taught me a lot. Amanda and I managed to remain on good terms. We decided to move on, but every now and then when we bumped into each other, she'd always manage a hello. It was comforting to know that there were no negative feelings, but I longed for the affection she'd once shown me.

THE EXPATRIATE

Paul Kange parked his taxi outside the international terminal at Jackson Airport. He squinted his eyes against the afternoon sun, watching a Boeing 747 that had just landed. It was half past four pm and many workers were clocking out for the day. Only a handful of airport staff and security guards manned the terminal entrance. Paul estimated that it would take about thirty minutes for the passengers to go through immigration checks before exiting the terminal.

Sitting in the soft driver's seat with the air conditioning on, his eyelids began to shut but he forced them open and sat up straight. Paul shook his head several times but the fatigue remained. Using his palms, he pressed hard on his eyelids trying to rub the sleep away. His day had started at five am as usual and he could feel the fatigue catching up on him.

For Paul, making ends meet was tough. He'd been a taxi driver for over five years now. Paul worked seven days a week to support his family and to pay the bills. Despite his hard work, he still struggled to put food on the table every day. On top of that were the never-ending customary obligations like his younger brother's bride price payment.

Thirty minutes passed and still no passengers came through the exit door. The immigration staff were always slow, Paul reassured himself. But he was starting to worry whether he'd make enough money to contribute to the bride price. His family back home in Hagen had planned to host the bride price ceremony at the end of the month. That was only a week away.

The international terminal was one of his favourite places to make extra money. Paul usually charged the expatriates double since they were not familiar with the regular taxi fares in Port Moresby. The expatriates had no problem in paying the taxi fares. Some were generous enough to give him additional tips for his friendliness.

Two other taxis pulled up beside him. It was a rat race to make money in the taxi business. Paul had to be one step ahead of the others.

At quarter past five, the passengers started coming out. Paul jumped out of the taxi and plastered a wide smile on his face. "Good evening," he greeted any expatriate that looked his way.

Most Australians seemed to like smiles. One of the expatriates, somewhere in his forties was Paul's guess, walked over to him. "Holiday Inn please."

"Sure, hop on," Paul said courteously.

The expatriate climbed in and closed the door. Paul put his passenger's suit case in the boot. A smile spread across his face knowing that he would make extra money.

"Sir, are you comfortable or should I lower the air conditioning?"

Paul asked when he was back behind the wheel.

The expatriate glanced up for a second from his phone. "I am fine, thanks."

Holiday Inn was a short drive if they used the fly-over and would cost only twenty kina. But if Paul used the other route from Six Mile to Five Mile and Boroko then back to Waigani, he could charge the expatriate fifty kina. Paul thought about it as he turned on the ignition. At the roundabout, Paul turned left towards Six Mile.

Paul had read somewhere that Australians liked to make friends and his experience mostly backed that up, though he never really knew how to make friends with them.

He glanced at his passenger from the rear view mirror. "How was your flight?"

"Not bad."

And that was that. Guess we're not talking, Paul thought. How do you know who wants to talk and who doesn't?

The awkward silence made Paul feel sleepy again and he had to swerve a little to stay in his lane. He switched on the radio to keep himself awake. The song *'Mt. Lamina'* by Wame Blood came on. Who could sleep with that song playing! Paul smiled to himself. Besides, the expatriate seemed to love it.

At the Five Mile roundabout, they continued towards Boroko. From there, they headed back towards Waigani. Some twenty minutes later, they arrived at the Holiday Inn.

Paul jumped out and ran around to open the boot. He retrieved the suitcase and brought it to the expatriate.

"Here's your baggage Sir. That would cost you fifty kina."

The expatriate held out a twenty kina note. *"Tenkiu stret wantok. Yu gat gutpla nait."*

Paul stood frozen in shock. He stared at the expatriate with a confused expression riddled on his face.

"You welcome Sir," he said, accepting the twenty kina note without protesting.

Back in the driver's seat, Paul placed the twenty kina note into his wallet and rubbed his forehead.

How did the expatriate know Tok Pisin? Was he a mixed-race or did he grow up in Papua New Guinea? Paul wondered as he watched the expatriate man walk off towards the hotel's reception.

What a waste of fuel for a lousy twenty kina! He sighed and closed his tired eyes for some minutes while waiting for the next passenger.

ONE HOUR SERVICE

The queue was getting longer and longer at the Immigration Office. The place was stuffy and with the unexpected power outage, the atmosphere was filled with frustration. One or two security personnel could be seen trying to keep the crowd under control.

There was nothing to do except wait. Some people had headphones and were listening to music. They seemed to be in another world, unaware of the sheer boredom others without such apparatus were going through. There were a few others reading newspapers. The airless atmosphere was an invitation for anyone to faint. Many of the people in the queue were complaining about the poor service.

The lady in front of me turned to chat with me. She looked furious and exhausted. "Do they have a standby generator?"

"Umm, they should have one. This is a government office."

"Too much loans and now the government has no money to buy fuel for the generator."

As a public servant, I felt somewhat guilty about her remark. "Yeah, the country's going through a tough time with a deficit budget."

"They should introduce an online system so we don't have to stand the whole day here. Forty two years after independence and we're still using manual systems."

I nodded. "Seriously. I have a lot of reports to complete in the office. But I desperately need my passport today."

"So, you travelling out of the country?"

"Yeah…"

I was nominated by my boss to attend an APEC meeting in Beijing the following week. As such, I had to provide a current passport to the Chinese Embassy because the Chinese government would fund my travel and accommodation.

My feet were killing me. The lack of seats added to the entire discomfort. I looked around and saw that everyone had the same shiny, sweaty faces and a resigned air to match. I managed to lean against the wall, making sure beforehand that it wasn't dirty.

After some time, the lights came on and those at the head of the queue moved up nearer towards the counters providing a sense of relief that the queue was getting shorter. A highlands man tried to push his way to the front and I stamped on his feet, giving him a furious look. "Follow the queue buddy! Who are you to take short-cuts?"

It was almost lunch time and the queue moved so slowly. In fact it just inched along at a snail's pace. There were about twenty people in front to me. To make matters worse, there were only two ladies at the counters when there were supposed to be five. I was already restless.

There was a notice on one of the counters in front of us with the immortal words printed on it 'PASSPORTS FOR SAME DAY PROCESSING: 8:00 AM – 12:00 PM'. That said everything.

Beside the counter with the notice there was a door which opened and a smartly dressed man walked out. He passed down the queue collecting passport applications from people who had paid for same day processing.

I handed him my passport application. "Sir, I need my passport by four o'clock please."

He examined it and moved on to the next person. He moved along the queue with a self-important air about him, as if he was the only worker at the Immigration Office and all the responsibility was on his shoulders.

Feeling somewhat relieved, I walked over to the market stalls outside the Central Government Office to grab a bite and some cigarettes before heading back to my office at Gordons. Some minutes later, the man from the Immigration Office came out for lunch too. He approached me with the same bleak expression on his face.

"Bro, you need your passport urgently right?"

"Yes. I have to submit it to Chinese Embassy tomorrow so they can sort out my travel immediately. I have to attend an APEC meeting in Beijing next week," I explained.

"I can sort it out for you but there's a few officers we have to please before they process your passport quickly."

"Uhmm okay. So how much to please them?"

"A hundred kina for lunch should do."

I stared at him blankly. "I just need my passport today."

Fortunately, I was paid my travelling allowance so I was loaded. I handed him a hundred kina note and gave him my mobile phone number.

He quickly hid the money in his pocket. "I'll call you when your passport is ready for pick up."

"Thanks. Please sort my passport as a top priority."

He gave a reassuring smile. "No worries. I'll call you."

An hour later, my mobile phone rang.

"Hello?" I quickly answered it.

"Hi bro. This is Moni Pes from the Immigration Office. Your passport is ready for pick up."

"Thanks. I'll be right on my way. That was fast!"

I drove back to the Immigration Office feeling jittery about what had just transpired. I knew it wasn't the most ethical thing to do but that is the way business is done in Papua New Guinea.

BUAI SELLER

The afternoon air was dry and humid as the scorching sun beat down mercilessly on old Kurabi's head. Another week of business not going well, but he was hoping to make more today than the previous days. It was two o'clock and traffic filled the small street from Lamana Hotel down to Holiday Inn - cars, buses and people were everywhere. He watched elegantly dressed men and women in suits walk in and out of their offices.

Kurabi was in his early fifties and had spent over twenty years in the betel nut trade, saving every little profit he made, making provision for the future. He dreamed of the day he would purchase a Toyota Coaster bus and start his own registered PMV business. Perhaps, his son would be a lawyer one day. Sweat beaded on his forehead. Kurabi wiped the sweat with his palms. His back suffered the most as he had to spend the whole day sitting under the neem trees opposite the Aopi Building which housed the National Department of

Health office. With a carton of betel nut in front of him, he could feel the fatigue in his body. But his mind was far away.

Kurabi remembered coming to Port Moresby in the early 1980s as a young man in search of opportunities to find employment and help his parents back at home in the cold mountains of Ialibu in the Southern Highlands province. An uncle of his who lived in the city had told him stories of all the high-rise buildings, lots of cars, people, Asian companies and lots of opportunities to be employed. He sold enough coffee from his small plantation and bought a one-way plane ticket to Port Moresby to live with his relatives at Tete squatter settlement on the outskirts of Gerehu suburb. Tete settlement was a no-go zone for most city residents because of the high rate of criminal activities. But for the highlanders living there, it was home.

For the next five years he went from office to office, asking for employment as a cleaner, gardener or even as a casual laborer. But fortune had never smiled on Kurabi since he couldn't read and write and had no formal education.

Kurabi fell in love with a woman from Simbu who also lived at the settlement with her family. After some fooling around they had their first child, a boy. Three years later, a daughter followed. Because of that, he started selling betel nuts to make ends meet for his impoverished family.

On favorable days, he would make over two hundred kina. He would use a hundred kina to buy new stock from the Mekeo and Kerema suppliers who usually sold a ten-kilogram bag of betel nut for twenty kina. The remaining money would be used for food and sustenance. He also managed to pay for his children's school fees with the little money he made.

That was how Kurabi survived in Port Moresby until the Governor for the National Capital District introduced the Betel Nut Control Law in 2013. Although the ban was effective, people in Port Moresby still loved chewing betel nut.

Why stop the trading of *buai* when the Government can't create jobs for everyone, he thought bitterly.

"How much for your *buai*?"

Someone disturbed Kurabi from his reverie. He looked up to see a pretty Papuan woman with a very shapely figure. She was young, probably in her early twenties he judged, and smartly dressed for an office job.

"Only one kina. Fresh, meaty *buai*," he replied.

She pulled out a two kina note and bent over to pick up two betel nuts and mustard from the carton that Kurabi placed in front him. His eyes focused on her cleavage and firm breasts. The view was phenomenal.

She chewed one betel nut and stood for a while before walking off. Her short, tight black skirt gave a perfect outline of her fine assets. Kurabi watched her buttocks swaying from side to side with every step she took. He felt himself getting aroused. This old thing is still kicking, he thought with a mischievous smile.

"Damn! Such a hottie!"

A young man standing nearby said to his friends. It seemed like Kurabi was not the only one who'd been distracted by the Papuan lady's ass. The young man looked like he was from the Sepik area. He was with a group of men, all smartly dressed too, probably on their afternoon break. They came over, placed a twenty kina note and collected ten betel nuts.

"Is she married?" the same young man asked.

"I wouldn't know. Why don't you ask her yourself?" his friend said and they started laughing.

Kurabi could understand a little English and joined in the conversation. "Sorry son, that's for businessmen only."

The Sepik bloke grimaced. "Very true."

Kurabi found a ten kina note from his waist bag and gave the young men their change. Judging from the weight of the waist bag, Kurabi had probably made more than two hundred kina. There were two other betel nut sellers to compete with so he was lucky. He thought of buying a packet of lamb flaps and some vegetables from the market to take home for dinner tonight. His children would have some pocket money for school tomorrow. His wife also wanted to buy more wool to complete her *bilums* to sell.

What more could he ask for? So long as he had a roof over his head, a happy family and children attending school, life wasn't so bad after all. Today was one of his good days. He smiled, feeling somewhat happy with a sense of satisfaction at the day's earnings.

He wiped more sweat on his forehead with his shirt and shielded his eyes from the sun. It was only an hour to go before four o'clock when the Government employees would finish work and Kurabi would also be on his way home.

Suddenly, out of the corner of his eyes, he saw a blue Toyota Land Cruiser speeding down from the Lamana Hotel road heading towards him. Kurabi knew that it was none other than the Police or the National Capital District Commission law enforcers.

Kurabi quickly poured all the betel nuts from the carton into his *bilum* and tried to escape by running up a small hill.

The vehicle was already very close and several policemen jumped out from the back and started running after him.

"Holim em!" a policeman's voice yelled.

Kurabi had witnessed how the police beat up betel nut sellers they caught and so he ran with all the speed his old legs could carry him. The other two betel nut sellers were younger than him so they were already at the top of the hill.

Turning his head slightly, he looked back to see if the policemen were catching up. Kurabi ran with all his might.

'Please Lord, I don't want to be caught,' he kept praying.

One of the newly recruited policemen caught up with Kurabi and grabbed him by the shirt. "Stop right there!"

The policeman grabbed Kurabi and landed a fist on the side of his face. Kurabi's hands flew up to block more punches to his face but was too late. Another punch on his head made him momentarily unconscious and he fell backwards to the ground. Kurabi blinked hard as his vision slowly returned.

Kurabi cried out in pain and rolled over to protect his face. His head was thumping. Another stocky policeman kicked him in the stomach with his boots.

"How many times will we stop you people from selling betel nut in public areas?"

Kurabi felt a sharp pain in his side. One of his ribs might have snapped. He begged the policemen to stop.

"Get his *bilum* and destroy all the *buai!*" the Senior Constable commanded. "The waist bag too!"

The Senior Constable was a bulky man. He had a potbelly so he was the last one to catch up with the other two policemen.

"No! Please don't take my money!" Kurabi protested in pain and tried to stagger onto his feet but couldn't.

Another fist smashed into Kurabi's face and he flopped onto his side. He didn't move. An explosion of pain shot up through his body. He laid there crying as the policemen ripped the waist bag and *bilum* off him. They poured out all the betel nuts and by standers rushed for the scattered betel nuts. Kurabi's waist bag containing the days taking which also disappeared.

"Go home now and don't ever sell *buai* again!" the Senior Constable ordered. "If we catch you again, you'll be thrown in jail!"

With that, the three policemen returned to their vehicle and drove off laughing at the old man. The confiscated money would be used to buy their beer. That was what the policemen where known for in Papua New Guinea.

Kurabi slowly rolled onto his hands to push himself up onto his feet. He was still dizzy and couldn't breathe. He stumbled and blinked hard. It felt like lightning bolts were shooting down his back. Slowly, he moved his leg, trying to figure out if it was broken or not. It hurt, but he could still move.

A kind young man helped Kurabi to his feet. He then bought a bottle of water and gave it to Kurabi to drink.

"Thank you," Kurabi murmured.

"Bloody grade ten dropouts who think they're above the law!" the young man swore at the policemen.

Kurabi's face and knees were covered in bruises and his whole body was sore. He couldn't stop shaking. Tears ran down his cheeks. All his hard work that day had been in vain.

Cursing silently, he rubbed the tears and blood on his face with his shirt then poured some water onto his face and drank the rest.

He sat down under the tree lost in thought for a long time. What will my family have for dinner tonight? His mind was numb. He just sat there, trying to feel better. He had dreams and ambitions just like everyone else.

More tears started to form in his eyes.

OFFICE AFFAIR

Dr. Meri Pes rubbed his eyes tiredly and then returned to the stack of reports before him. He checked his watch, it was a little after six o'clock. Dr. Meri Pes sat down on his desk thinking of Barbie Tuks, the Senior Executive Assistant for the Secretary. They had planned to go out for dinner after all the staff had left the office. It would be the source of office gossip if other staff knew, and could taint his reputation and cost him his job too. He'd had a number of extramarital affairs, enough that the prospect of another woman in his bed produced only anticipation, but the way he felt would not be described as mild.

Whatever it was about Barbie, he wanted her. He thought of the way she walked, her petite build and slender hips moving in a way that made sweat pop out on his forehead. Barbie was in her early fifties, but still looked good. It would take a while for him to tire of her.

Although in his late fifties, Dr. Meri Pes still maintained a solid figure and still had hair on his head. Most men his age were already bald. He was also tall, with eyes that made women his age go a little crazy.

Dr. Meri Pes had joined the newly established Department of Communication and Technology as the Deputy Secretary a few months ago. Before that he was senior lecturer at the University of Technology in Lae.

The Department of Communication and Technology had arranged for temporary accommodation at the Gateway Hotel for him while he sorted out his permanent accommodation. Housing in the nation's capital Port Moresby was a serious problem, so it would take a while before a decent house could be found. This meant that his wife, children and grandchildren would have to remain in Lae until the housing issue was resolved.

After two broken marriages, Barbie Tuks no longer had so many stars in her eyes. She struggled on her own to raise her four grown up children and one grandchild. She knew the danger she was in but was attracted to his money and wanted a quick promotion in her job.

Dr. Meri Pes glanced at his watch again. It was almost thirty minutes past six. He and Barbie had clicked on the first day he started work with the Department. They had had several dinner dates and she spent some nights with him in his hotel room. He felt a little guilty for doing this behind his wife's back. But everything about Barbie felt magical.

His wife for thirty years, Linda was a very loving mother of their children, a homemaker and a Sunday school teacher at their local Lutheran church and a loving and devoted wife.

But all of that aside, Barbie Tuks was a sensual woman and he couldn't resist her charms. He didn't want any rumors about his extramarital affair to leak out.

He shut down his laptop and was about to pack up for the day when Barbie entered his office.

"Right on time," he said.

"Sorry to keep you waiting, Doctor."

He gave her a cheeky smile. "No, it's all good. Let's go."

His car was a luxurious Hyundai Tucson, the latest model on the market. After helping her into the car, he walked around to the driver's seat and got behind the wheel.

"I was thinking of dinner at Fugui Restaurant. You okay with that?"

"Sure," she replied feeling the warmth in his voice.

Barbie thoroughly approved of the restaurant he'd chosen. It was a fancy Japanese restaurant that served delicious seafood. The interior was dim, the diners were discretely isolated and the music was slow sentimental songs played at a pleasant volume.

On arrival, they were shown to a private room. The dining table was small, so that when they were seated their knees touched. Their eyes met across the table, and a slow sleepy smile touched his lips and made his eyelids droop heavily.

Dr. Meri Pes ordered dinner and wine and throughout the meal he continued staring at her. Inevitably, they talked about work, since that was the common ground for them. He was quite knowledgeable in all aspects of ICT.

He charmed her, making her feel appreciated, something she hadn't felt in a long time.

"We have to be discrete with our relationship,' he said with a concerned tone.

"Don't worry, darling, we'll play it safe."

Every time her dark lashes teased and he saw the wicked glint in her eyes, he felt his body tighten with need.

"Finish your food," he said gently.

Despite the way he made her feel shaky inside, she smiled at him. "I can't. You're staring at me."

"I'm sorry. I can't keep my eyes away from you." His voice was tender and low.

They finished their main courses and the waiter cleared the dishes away as they lingered over the wine. Barbie had thought that she wouldn't be able to eat any dessert, but when the waiter brought the dessert cart, she stared at the vanilla ice cream until her mouth was watering.

"I'll have the ice cream. Would you like some?" she offered.

"It's okay. I'll just have coffee."

Barbie certainly enjoyed the food. She looked up and caught his gaze, and smiled as she read his thoughts. "Take it easy with that look. I might faint."

He laughed with desire in his eyes. "You ready to leave?"

"Yes, darling. I'm done."

Dr. Meri Pes took her arm as they walked back out to his car. Barbie quivered. She felt mesmerized, totally unable to move away from him. She was overwhelmed by his manly touch.

He parked the car at the Gateway Hotel car park. Without a word, he bent his head and covered her lips with his mouth no longer able to control his desire. Dr. Meri Pes was too absorbed in the moment and unaware that a security guard, who happened to be a cousin brother of his wife, was watching them.

"Let's go to my room," he ordered.

Barbie quivered against him, well aware of his need. She wanted him too.

Two hours later, he dropped Barbie off at her house at Waigani and returned back to his hotel room. He jumped straight into bed, but his subconscious mind played the night for him again.

What a night, he thought and smiled.

Linda couldn't believe what her cousin in Port Moresby had told her over the phone. Sweat started forming on her forehead. Her heart was pounding so fast. Linda had been hurt before, but this one cut her deep. She sat still and went pale like a statue, feeling a lump in her throat.

The thought of her husband jumping into bed with another woman drove her mad. She wanted to smash all the kitchen utensils. But her children were fast asleep and so she decided against it. She didn't want to disturb them.

All these years, she was the only person who had stood by his side through thick and thin. She found a part-time job to support him when he was away in Australia pursuing further studies for a Masters and PhD at the Australian National University.

How could he do that to me, she thought angrily.

It felt like a thousand swords stabbing her and the wound would linger with her for the rest of her life. She sat in the chair and cried for a long time, not knowing what to do.

She slowly wiped the tears from her eyes. Her emotions swung from hurt and pain to raw fury. And then to a cold determination to take revenge.

No way am I going to let both of them have a good time. I'll make sure they end up in court and lose their jobs, she thought.

The thought of them fired from work gave Linda a sense of relief. She had to play it cool and catch them unaware. She'd catch the next flight she could get to Port Moresby.

A quick look at the clock told her that it was almost three-thirty in the morning. She forced herself back to sleep, but woke up early, eager to get things moving.

Dr. Meri Pes was at his office table a little early and his Executive Assistant Ranu made him a cup of coffee. He took the coffee gratefully.

"Thanks Ranu. I missed breakfast this morning."

His mobile phone rang. He checked to see who was calling and saw that it was his wife, Linda. He went back into his office and closed the door.

"Hello honey," he answered sweetly.

Linda paused for a while. All the pain and anger of betrayal made her entire body shake. She wanted to scream and swear at him but kept her nerves in check.

"Morning, just checking on you," she said calmly. "The kids miss you."

"Oh, I miss all of you," he sounded genuine, but deep down he knew it was a lie.

"When is the Department going to sort our accommodation so we can come over to Port Moresby?" she asked.

"Soon, I promise. I'll talk to the Director for Finance and Administration again to hurry things along," he reassured her.

"Okay, I miss you too," she felt tears form in her eyes. "Hope you're not doing anything silly there?"

"I'm good, honey," he chuckled to hide the guilt.

"Well, you take care of yourself, okay?" she said and hung up.

Dr. Meri Pes pondered for a while. He did miss his wife but the taste of another woman's body delighted him more. She couldn't give him the satisfaction that Barbie was giving. He wasn't in a rush to relocate his wife and children to Port Moresby just yet.

What you don't know won't hurt you! The expression popped into his head. It was something he read somewhere. It wasn't exactly a Biblical scripture but maybe there was some truth to it. Well, Linda doesn't know so it can't hurt her, he thought

He picked his mobile phone again and typed a message before sending it to Barbie's cellphone.

"Lunch at Duffy?" he asked, more like proposed.

A few minutes later, his phone vibrated with a reply. "Sure darling."

A sense of elated satisfaction came over him as he thought of lunch with Barbie.

At lunchtime, Dr. Meri Pes came out of his office. Barbie was waiting for him at the main door leading to the lift. He entered the lift without even saying a word to her. It was part of their tactic to act normal so colleagues at the office would not be suspicious of anything going on between them.

The Secretary, Professor Save Mahn, joined them in the lift. Professor Save Mahn was a tall man in his early sixties with some grey hair on his head, the country's leading ICT expert and a respected man. He was always conscious about his diet and maintained a trim build.

The Secretary and Dr. Meri Pes started chatting about the strategic plan that the staff in the Planning Division were working on.

"Dr. Meri Pes, please follow up with the policy and planning staff and get them to complete the strategic plan. We need to finalize the document and submit it to the National Executive Council in the next Parliamentary sitting," the Secretary said with a hint of urgency in his voice.

"I'll meet with the Director after lunch and inform you on the status of the document," Dr. Meri Pes reassured the Secretary.

At the ground floor exit, Linda paced back and forth at the visitors counter and stood uneasily at the sight of her husband. She figured that the lady among them was none other than the bitch. She had only one piece of hand luggage with her and had caught a taxi straight from the airport to the Department of Higher Education office.

Dr. Meri Pes froze for a moment as if he'd seen a ghost. He couldn't believe his eyes. He held his breath, totally dumbfounded by his wife's presence. Linda confronted them. Her eyes were bloodshot and full of rage.

"So, this is the *pamuk* lady you've been screwing around with?" Linda asked her husband in an angry tone while staring at Barbie.

She was shaking with anger. Professor Save Mahn gave a quizzical look at Dr. Meri Pes, not knowing what was going on.

"Linda? Calm down please. When did you get here and what's the matter?" Dr. Meri Pes asked, still looking confused.

Linda carefully watched her husband's reaction and it was painfully obvious on his face that he was hiding something.

"You and Barbie have been screwing around. People saw you two together and told me so I had to come over. That's the matter!" she shouted at the top of her lungs.

Dr. Meri Pes stood there mute, not knowing what to say or do next. Colleagues on their way out for lunch and employees from other nearby offices started flocking over to watch the commotion. Barbie was embarrassed and started to walk away. Linda instantly grabbed Barbie by the hair and pulled her back.

Barbie was trembling in fear and tried to pull away from Linda's grasp. "Let me go, please!"

"*Pamuk*, shut the fuck up!" Linda punched her in the jaw. "Bloody *pamuk*! You're a whore who goes opening her legs to bosses! What a shame! Useless lady!"

Linda tore Barbie's dress and with her right fist, she punched Barbie over and over in the face, splitting her lips and nose. Barbie tried to escape but couldn't.

Dr. Meri Pes grabbed Linda's arms to stop the fight. "Can we solve this issue as adults please," he begged his wife.

"What's there to solve? I am taking both of you to court for adultery! This old *pamuk* needs to learn a lesson not to fool around with another lady's husband!"

Linda kept screaming. Barbie finally pulled away with blood dripping from her mouth and nose.

Realizing that it was a marital issue, Professor Save Mahn walked away and pulled out his cell phone to call the police hotline.

The shouting and cursing from Linda continued, as she went on and on about Barbie being a gold digger and home wrecker until a police vehicle pulled up at the office car park. It felt good to finally beat the day lights out of Barbie and boy did it feel good to get that off her chest. Linda had so much she wanted to say, but just stood there smirking. She felt proud of herself though at the very least.

"You two ladies and sir, please get in the vehicle now. We'll sort this out at the Police Station," a policeman ordered.

Dr. Meri Pes was late for work two days later. He looked tired and wasn't beaming as usual. He felt somewhat powerless. He had made a fool of himself and now the whole office was talking about him, he thought bitterly. Even his Executive Assistant Ranu looked at him as if he was a piece of trash.

He logged in to his email account and skimmed through the new emails. A letter on his table caught his attention. It was his termination letter for breaching the Public Service General Orders and also his contract of employment. The Secretary requested that he clear his table and return his vehicle keys by close of business. He was also given a week to vacate the room at the hotel.

Dr. Meri Pes went blank with shock. With his personal life in chaos, that was the final straw. It was too much for him to digest at the moment. He threw the laptop to the floor.

"No, no, no way! I can't be terminated! I've contributed a lot to the Department. Damn it!"

He swallowed heavily, feeling his pulse quickening and his palms began to sweat. The extramarital affair had landed him in court for adultery and termination from his job! He started feeling a splitting headache.

Dr. Meri Pes took a deep breath and started clearing his table. He decided to put his anger and ego aside and accept the consequences of his stupidity.

It was his last day at work as the Deputy Secretary for the Department of Communication and Technology.

BOAT GIRL

Daru town was peaceful at this time of the night with just a handful of stars in the sky. There were only a few lights that flickered on and off on the empty street. The sea breeze gently rustled the leaves in the trees. Not one prowling house cat was in sight. Jess stood beside the street near her house puffing a cigarette.

She was a twenty-two year old single mother of two kids from different men. But she still looked good. She was slim with a trim waist, firm breasts and a to-die-for ass wrapped in tight jeans. Her white top was silky and almost see through. She sprayed herself lightly with her favorite perfume from her handbag.

To most people, it would have been late, but for her, the night was still young. Her eyes silently scanned the empty street. She wasn't afraid of the darkness.

As a teenager, Jess had dreams of graduating from high school and attending university to become a journalist. But all her dreams were torn to shreds when her father died while she was still in high school. Her family suffered from the constant struggle to make ends meet. At such a harsh time, all their relatives turned their backs and closed their doors to Jess and her mother.

As the eldest of three children, Jess assumed the role of the caretaker in her family. She had to support her siblings while her mother eked out a living selling ice blocks and scones. Her mother was a hard-working lady, but her ice block sales didn't generate enough money to pay for school fees, food and other necessities.

Jess's grade ten education was not enough to find her a job. Besides, there were hardly any major companies in Daru and employment opportunities were scarce. She was left with no choice but to frequent the New Century hotel at night as a prostitute. She fell pregnant to two of her clients, both sailors from the Steamship Shipping company barges that visited Daru occasionally.

Every night she would leave the house with hopes that one day a good man would marry her and take care of her and her children. She wouldn't have to sell her body for money any more. Every morning when she returned, she would cry quietly. That wasn't the life she wanted. At least, however, she made enough money to buy food and pay for her siblings' school fees.

"Same shit, different day," Jess murmured, lit another cigarette and puffed deeply.

The effect of the nicotine brought some relief as she strolled towards the New Century hotel down at the beachfront, within walking distance from her house. She was a familiar face at the hotel. The security guards at the front gate always let her through without asking any questions. Daru was a small town and everyone knew each other quite well.

Jess drifted in quietly avoiding a group of drunkards who were causing a nuisance. She found a stool at the corner of the bar. A local song was playing at a pleasant volume. The bar was not too crowded. The only men there were Papua New Guinea Defense Force soldiers from the navy ship that was in port. They were having a good time and making lots of noise. Jess ordered a glass of wine and sipped it slowly to pass time. Several of the soldiers started eyeing her. Noticing them, Jess licked her lips and flicked her hair back over her shoulder provocatively to entice them.

A uniformed soldier in his forties glanced at Jess from the other side of the bar. She returned the glance. After about five minutes, the bartender brought Jess another glass of wine. Jess had not ordered it and the bartender said it was from the gentleman across the bar. She looked across the bar at the uniformed soldier, smiled and gave a nod of her head to say thank you.

At this point the man got up from his seat, walked across to Jess's side of the bar and sat in the barstool next to her

"Hi pretty lady, you on your own?"

"Yes. Just me, myself and I," she chuckled with a wry smile and glanced up at him.

He was tall with a muscular, athletic build.

"What are you having?"

"Red wine," she replied.

He ordered himself a stubby and red wine for Jess. "What's your name, pretty?"

"Jess," she said and flashed a smile at him.

He introduced himself. Peter was his name and he was from East Sepik. He was the ship's commander, based at Murray Barracks in Port Moresby. Jess and Peter continued chatting for about thirty minutes with several hearty laughs mixed in.

"Hey, your buddies might be wondering what you're up to," she said after a while.

He ordered another round of stubby and wine. "Don't worry about them. They're enjoying their beer."

Jess could tell by the look in Peter's eyes that he was pretty into her. She was also feeling tipsy from the wine.

She wasn't an amateur. This was her game and she had to take control. Jess stood up from her barstool and moved between Peter's knees and closer to him as he sat in his bar stool.

"I know you want to bang me so bad, don't you?" Jess whispered in his ear.

Peter felt himself getting excited. "Umm, yes baby…"

She placed her hand on his thigh and smiled. Peter did not seem to object. As she did, it was clear by looking at the bulge in his pants that Peter was enjoying it. Jess then ran her hand down the length of the bulge, down between his legs and back up. She repeated this several times as she moved her body closer to his.

"Two hundred kina and you can bang me all you want," she whispered and looked directly into his eyes.

Peter was already in a highly aroused state and couldn't turn down the offer. He stood up and removed his wallet from his back pocket and handed Jess two hundred in notes. She put it into her handbag and they got up and left the bar.

There was a small bed in his tiny cabin on the naval ship. Peter removed his uniform in an instant and then ripped away Jess's clothes and forced her to the bed. She'd learnt not to reject any man, but Peter was quite rough. She was used to this kind of man, the kind that wanted to dominate a woman. So she lay back on the bed and spread her legs for him.

"You better use a condom. I don't want to get pregnant," she ordered him. She had learn her lesson the hard way and didn't want another fatherless child.

Peter quickly put on a condom and rammed her like a raging bull. Jess closed her eyes and tried to imagine other things to distract her mind. She always kept her emotions under control.

This isn't love, just business as usual. It will all be over soon, she reminded herself.

He groaned loudly and quickened his pace.

Jess thought about her father. The memories of her late father flashed vividly in her mind, as she remembered his words full of wisdom. Nothing comes easy in life. You just have to work hard, and success will be yours. That was one of the many pieces of advice given to her by her father. She missed him dearly.

Peter finally climaxed and lay down beside her exhausted. Jess got out of bed and put on her clothes. It was already day break and she needed to get home to shower and rest. She was exhausted too. She pulled out a cigarette from her handbag.

"I need to smoke," she muttered.

"You'll have to go up to the deck to smoke."

"Okay, I'll be off then. Smoke and head home. Thanks for everything," she said politely and left his cabin.

Arriving home, Jess put her handbag on the old table, the only furniture they had in their run down house. She took out the two hundred kina notes from the bag and held it in her hands. Her son, Junior, woke up and start crying. "Mummy, I'm hungry."

"Go eat some scones that grandma baked and let mummy get some rest. I'll go to the shop in the afternoon and buy chocolate biscuits for you, I promise," Jess replied impassively.

"I want chocolate biscuits!" Junior glared at her and shouted in a high-pitched voice.

His voice shrilled through the house. He was extremely stubborn and adamant. And, needless to say, when he demanded something, that 'something' must be provided to him as soon as possible. Otherwise, he would throw a tantrum.

"Oh God! Junior! Stop it! Enough is enough!" Jess screeched in anger, suddenly losing her calm.

Junior burst out crying. Wearing a pitiful expression, she soothed him.

"Oh my baby! Stop crying. Mummy is sorry. You know I'll do anything for you." She gave him a tight hug.

For Jess, life was hell. However, she could not run away from the problems life brought her. She had to face them.

Her children meant the world to her. Jess loved them so much but she had nothing left in her broken body to give them. Her body was exploited and her soul had ripped apart long ago. All she had left was a heart that was pure.

Life can be a bitch sometimes. Jess sighed. Well, it beats selling ice blocks for a living, she thought to herself.

PUBLIC SERVANT

The office was in a mess with papers and files all over the place. Jayden sat at his desk putting things in a proper order. It was not easy, but he had nearly completed doing it.

He walked over to the wall where a multi-drawered filing cabinet stood. Slowly and carefully he picked up each pile and placed it in the corresponding drawer. It took him about thirty minutes and he looked pleased with himself. Jayden looked at the clock. It was eleven fifty-three, almost time for lunch.

He loved his job with the Research Council and looked forward to coming in every day, especially since his recent appointment as the Director of the Project Management division. The management had recognized his talents and had promoted him. Jayden was a smart man. With a degree in accounting and management and almost ten years of work experience with the private sector and Australian Aid development programs, he had slowly climbed the corporate ladder.

He enjoyed the feeling of being the boss. It was nice having a team who had to listen to him and do as he said. But it came with a price at times. If he didn't step in and make sure the project reports were completed promptly, the Chief Executive Officer would be after him.

Still, he loved his job as a public servant. A government job was better than a job with the private sector because it was stable, secure, fairly paid, and generally flexible. Without it, he'd never been able to give his small family a decent life. And besides, he noted wryly, he wouldn't have had the chance to travel overseas and attend meetings and meet a lot of people from many different walks of life.

Jayden was happy because it was Wednesday and that the weekend was close. It was also payday for the Government employees. He smiled to himself and looked at the time once more.

Twelve o'clock. Lunch time.

"Boss, I completed the project report that you requested," Mary, the Project Officer said to him when he was on his way out of the office.

"Ok, thanks. Leave it on my table. I've have a look at it when I return."

Jayden had watched Mary at work. She was very efficient and professional in carrying out her duties.

He strolled over to the nearest Bank South Pacific ATM around the corner and stood in the queue for a long time to check his balance. He was disappointed that his salary had not yet been credited to his account. Jayden pushed the glass door of the ATM room vehemently and darted out.

There were probably some delays in the banking system. It would come in soon. He was positive.

Jayden bought a cigarette from a street vendor and puffed on it before returning to the office. He had lots of work to be completed.

When he got back to the office, Jayden quickly logged onto his MacBook and checked his emails. He had sent an email to Christine, the Human Resource Officer to provide his pay slip for the current fortnight. She hadn't replied yet.

He wanted to confirm the deductions made from his salary. He had two outstanding loans from Moni Plus Limited and Teachers Savings and Loans Society. He calculated that about K600.00 would be deducted.

As he was doing the mental calculations, his phone rang. It was from none other than his mother. He dreaded the call because he knew that she would request some money.

It was ironic though. None of his family and relatives ever bothered to ring him or send a text message during business week. But on government pay week, his phone was like a hotline. It had become a ritual.

The noisy ringtone on his phone kept ringing.

"Yes mum, how are you?" he answered.

"Hello son. We are okay. How's work?"

"Same old, same old. Plenty of reports to complete."

"Son, your uncles are here from the village and there's not enough food in the house. I want them to return home over the weekend. Can you send us K300.00 please?"

His parents lived in Alotau. Although they were employed at the Alotau Provincial Hospital, they would often run short due to the endless visits from relatives from the village. Village people seem to think money grows on trees. Jayden was the only one that had a job with a good salary.

Jayden sighed. He was already annoyed. "My goodness! I am still repaying my loans mum! I have my rentals to pay too! Can't you people give me a break?"

"Sorry son, but we really need your help please," she kept pleading.

"Okay, okay, I'll send it over when my pay comes into my account!"

"Thank you son."

Jayden found it hard to turn down requests from his family. That often angered his wife, Carol, and they'd had many heated arguments in the past. Carol was half West Papua and West Sepik and although she had the looks of a West Papuan, she was short tempered like the Sepik people.

Who do they think you are? Santa Claus? Or some tycoon? Carol would argue that everyone had their own burdens to worry about and that they had a daughter to raise. She had a point.

He checked his WhatsApp messages and there was another request from his small sister Leino for some money to buy her shoes for school.

Jayden leaned back in his chair angered by the phone call and message. His family was a major liability. Every payday, for nine years now, they seemed to have some problem, emergency, burden or family crises. He was fed up. They didn't even seem to understand that he had his own family to worry about. Besides, the cost of living in Port Moresby was so high and he often had to borrow money to survive.

He picked up the report that Mary had placed on his table and flipped through quickly. A message tone beeped. He looked at his phone.

His anger evaporated within split-seconds when he saw that it was a BSP Pay Alert SMS that read:

Your account XXXXXX1045 was deposited with more than K50.00. Call *131*1# to check your account.

Jayden's gross pay was a little over K2,800.00 but K700.00 was deducted for tax and superannuation. Then another K600.00 deducted for his loan repayments leaving him with a net pay of K1,500.00.

Jayden had phone banking activated on his phone so he entered his password and transferred K400.00 to his mother's account. K100.00 was for Leino's shoes. He sent a text message to Leino to inform her that he had transferred the money to mum's account. He had K1,100.00 left in his account.

He still had his rentals and owed the highlands lady that sold betel nuts next door to his apartment some money. Jayden sighed and returned back to his fortnightly status report that he was working on the previous day. He edited it and added more information. Finally satisfied that his report was complete, he printed it out and signed.

"Please submit our division's report to the CEOs office," he instructed Mary politely. She nodded in compliance.

Jayden walked over to the staff tea room and poured himself a cup of coffee. It was three forty-five and he had a quarter of an hour to go before leaving the office. His mind wandered back to his family affairs. They barely survived from fortnight to fortnight. Carol was unemployed and his daughter Jodie was attending Sunny Bunny Kindergarten School, an expensive private school. The loans that he was repaying were for her school fees. To him, his daughter deserved the best education.

He finished his coffee. It was six past four now and colleagues started leaving the office.

Jayden pulled into the main road towards Boroko, which was quite busy at this time of the day. Everyone wanted to get home quickly from work. Jayden stepped hard on the brakes suddenly and jammed on the horn as a taxi changed lanes sharply in front without any signal and almost causing a collision.

"Bloody asshole! Do you know how to drive?" he shouted angrily. "Bloody highlands idiots! You think you own the road."

It didn't make the taxi driver look around, but at least it gave him the chance to vent his frustration.

The Pacific Real Estate office closed at five o'clock so Jayden accelerated and overtook the taxi. He was fortunate the Research Council subsidized two-thirds of his apartment rentals. He paid only K600.00 for rentals every fortnight. Jayden got to the real estate office in the nick of time.

"Last customer before you close for the day please," he begged the security guard to get in.

"Ok, make it quick," the guard ordered.

Jayden used his credit card to pay the rentals and was given a receipt. He drove over to Vision City to use the ATM to withdraw the remaining K500.00 in his account. Traffic was congested from Vision City to the Waigani traffic lights. So many things were running through his mind but, mainly, he was worried about his wife and daughter. What will he tell

Carol? How will they survive until the next fortnight? He pondered as he followed the slow moving traffic.

Jayden stopped by the neighbor's house and repaid the highlands lady with K300.00. He had borrowed K200.00 but she charged an interest of fifty percent. Such informal lenders were seriously ripping off working people with their ridiculous interest rates.

With only K200.00 left in his pocket, he headed home feeling exhausted and bankrupt. For almost a decade, he had lived with the same financial pressure from his family.

Does it ever end? He sighed. Jayden knew that a nasty argument awaited him at home.

GIRLS NIGHT OUT

Hannah studied herself in the mirror carefully. Her cleavage was showing nicely and she looked really hot. She smiled to herself. Hannah was a twenty-five year old flight attendant with Air Niugini. She wore a tight, black dress with a long slit on the side that revealed her thighs and shiny black leather heels. To finish off her look, she put on a maroon lipstick. Her curly hair and light brown complexion were the result of her parents' mixed background. Her mother was from Central and her father was from Milne Bay. She had noticed several of the male pilots gawking at her ass as she strode through the aisle of the aircraft. She was sexy and she knew it.

She checked herself out once more and giggled to herself with a weird expression of self-love. "Perfect!"

Hannah was excited. It was Friday night and, since Phil was out of the country, she had planned to hang out with her girlfriend Pauline. Pauline was a flight attendant also. She picked up her Samsung Galaxy S10 phone and sent a WhatsApp message to Pauline. "Bitch, are you ready?"

"Yeah," Pauline replied.

"Come over to my unit then."

Five minutes later there was a knock on Hannah's door. Hannah opened the door to let Pauline in. They lived in different flats at the Air Niugini Village at Korobosea.

Pauline was half Sepik and East New Britain, slim built and wore a tight-fitting, short black skirt exposing firm thighs that were nicely tanned. A pair of tall stilettos added to her height.

Hannah couldn't help admiring the way her ass swayed elegantly as she walked. It was obvious what the men at the airport were so keen to turn their heads to catch a glimpse of it.

"What do you think?" Pauline asked twirling round and smoothing the short skirt over her bum.

"Damn! You look hot, bitch. We should take a selfie to post on Facebook," Hannah winked.

Pauline laughed. "Oh bitch, we'll make the guys go crazy."

They twisted in a provocative pose, made fish lips and took several selfies on Hannah's phone camera. Hannah selected the best photo and posted it on her Facebook wall and tagged Pauline with the status: 'Girls just wanna have fun'. She put a wink emoticon after it.

Within minutes, her Facebook status got over fifty likes and some twenty comments from friends. Most were from young men saying how sexy they looked. One young man even sent her a message and asked for her number.

"Get lost, you loser!" Hannah replied and blocked him.

She was only interested in men with fancy vehicles and money because they could afford to take her out to the expensive hotels for dinner, spoil her with money and all the fine things in life.

Make up done, Hannah sprayed herself with her favorite perfume and they left for the Camry.

"Wow! Nice ride," Pauline exclaimed as she walked to the passenger seat.

It was Pauline's first time to ride in Hannah's new car. Hannah unlocked the car with the remote key and both of them got in. She turned on the engine and it came on silently. Hannah carefully reversed out and when she entered the main road, she accelerated.

"Wada Wow! Bad ass baby!" Pauline squealed.

Hannah laughed and overtook several vehicles on their way to Waigani. They started chatting about the latest gossip, which was a lot.

"So, whose ride is this?" Pauline asked looking curious.

Hannah wasn't sure about how to bring up the topic of Phil with her friend. She had been going around discretely with a politician but his wife found out and threatened her on Facebook. Hannah was embarrassed after that issue and kept a low profile for a while. Then, two weeks ago, she'd met Phil, an Australian businessman in his late fifties at the Gold Club. One thing quickly led to another that night and she found herself rubbing her ass up against his groin on the dance floor and having sex with him in a hotel suite. She had no idea how it happened. Phil bought her the Toyota Camry a few days ago as a present and had been transferring large sums of money to her account when she asked.

"Boyfriend's ride," she replied.

She didn't want to tell Pauline the whole truth, just enough for the moment. Pauline had some experience with older men too. She had gone out with a landowner from the LNG project in Tari once.

"Who is it?" Pauline kept pestering.

"Oh, just a man I met two weeks ago."

"Must be another politician again?"

Hannah raised her eyebrows, not wanting to be reminded of her past. She decided to spill the beans. "Well, he is an expatriate and much older than me."

"You are such a slut. He is married, isn't he?"

Hannah sighed. "Most probably, and over fifty."

"Damn! That's messed up. What are you going to do?"

Hannah looked worried. "That was what I was hoping you could help me out with."

"I am done with married men. It's too much sneaking around, and I don't like it. As far as the age difference, I guess I could live with that as long as he is decently fit, and doesn't try to be my dad, or worse, grandfather," Pauline joked.

Hannah laughed. "No, no, this guy is cool, for his age."

"Okay, then it's your decision if you want to be a home wrecker or not," Pauline quipped.

Hannah frowned looking disappointed.

"My advice is, stay away from him," Pauline cautioned her.

"Duly noted! We're young, wild and free bitch!" she winked at Pauline.

At the traffic light, Hannah leaned forward and turned on the car stereo. A favorite number was playing and they hummed softly while waiting for the traffic light to turn green, already feeling the Friday night party vibes.

The Cosmopolitan Club was filled to capacity that night. The club was brightly lit with strobe lights; a huge reflective ball was suspended over the dance floor and the music was deafening. There were about a dozen people dancing to the pulverizing techno beat. They would dissolve into a white smoke that shot out from the side of the dance floor.

Hannah was on her fifth glass of vodka and already feeling the effects of the alcohol. She walked over to the dance floor pulling Pauline along and started dancing provocatively. Out of the corner of her eye, she noticed a white dude. He was sitting at the bar with a drink in his hand and was watching her dance. Hannah's heart skipped a beat.

After the dance, they returned to their table and Hannah whispered to Pauline. "That white dude there kept staring at me when we were dancing."

She directed Pauline's attention to the expatriate.

"Oh My Gosh! He's so handsome! Go ask him for a dance before I do!" Pauline teased her.

"Nah, forget it," she felt a little guilty when she thought of Phil and exhaled in regret.

They ordered more glasses of martini and vodka. The night was getting groovier. Hannah took more photographs with her phone to upload on Facebook. The Cosmopolitan was the place where most big shots and businessmen hung out to celebrate an awesome week or to try to forget a miserable one.

Hannah jumped and quickly turned as a hand was placed on her shoulder. It was the white dude who had been staring at her when she was dancing.

"Hi, my name is Brett," he said in an English accent.

She smiled at him. "I am Hannah."

He was tall and had dark brown eyes. She saw her friend Pauline winking at her in encouragement.

"Would you like to dance with me?"

"I'd love to," she accepted.

They made their way through the crowded dance floor until they were in the middle. She pressed her body close to his and kept rubbing her hips and ass against him as they danced passionately. Hannah noticed that half the club was staring at them. She gave a little smile and kept dancing. Hannah loved attention. She was used to all of this. It was a lifestyle she'd become addicted to. Between music sets, they would head back to the table where he would buy her more drinks. She was having the time of her life.

Hannah headed for the bar to order more drinks. As she was waiting, she noticed a group of women staring at her across the bar. She noticed a familiar face among them and turned away. It was the wife of the politician she had fooled around with. Picking up her drinks she quickly made her way through the crowd back to the table.

Suddenly, Hannah felt someone grab her arm, and as she spun around, felt a punch in the face.

"So you're the slut who was fucking around with my hubby aye? Bloody slut! You're a home wrecker!" the woman yelled.

She punched Hannah viciously several times again in the face. Hannah lost her balance and fell onto the floor. Her nose was bleeding. Pauline came to her rescue and forced the lady to stop.

The club bouncers broke up the crowd that gathered around to see what was going on. Brett stood there looking confused about what had just happened.

"You two trouble makers, go home now!" one of the bouncers ordered them.

Hannah turned back to the politician's wife. "F**k you! I am not a home wrecker or a slut! Come anywhere near me again and I will call the Police!"

"That's enough Hannah! Let's get you home," Pauline snapped at her.

Pauline helped Hannah up to her feet and gave her some tissues to stop the bleeding. Hannah had a swollen, black eye and her nose was broken. The rest of her face was generally beaten up. Their night out ended up as a total disaster. They picked up their handbags before heading towards the door.

FACEBOOK ROMANCE

Dianne looked at the papers on her desk and sighed. She sorted them out into neat piles and checked them meticulously. There were letters, flyers and invitations to attend some meetings. It took her a while to sort them out in order of priority before sending them over to the General Manager's office. She then returned her attention to the computer to complete the letter to a client that she hadn't finished. It was only ten-thirty am and she'd complete the letter by lunchtime.

There was free Wi-Fi Internet access in the office so she quickly checked her Facebook account and notifications. She used a fake name 'Mummy Boss' on Facebook. A message notification popped up. It was from a Facebook friend by the name of 'Daddy Boss'. He sent morning greetings with a picture of a rose in the message. Dianne smiled.

"Oh, so sweet of you," she quickly typed him a reply.

Daddy Boss seemed to be a magnet for women on Facebook. His real name was William. He was some private lawyer and made a lot of money representing politicians in court. He wasn't a George Clooney look-alike, but ladies adorned his friend list because he flashed his sports car and cash on Facebook. Not a lot of males but many, many women. It wasn't something Dianne liked, but what could she do? Nothing. She was a married woman with a husband and son.

I must be out of my mind, she thought.

They had chatted several times. He seemed friendly. However, she never asked him any embarrassing questions about his private life. Was he married? Did he have kids?

Another message appeared. "So how's your day going?"

"Bored here," she replied.

"Oh, now that's a worry. How can I entertain you?"

"I don't know. What type of entertainment do you have in mind?" she typed back with a wink.

"What's your number?"

Dianne just stared at the screen, feeling a little nervous. Did he just ask for her number? She barely knew him and he already wants her number.

Before she could reply back, he typed again. "Can I have your number?"

She stared at the words, not knowing how to respond. Finally, she typed. "Sorry, I can't give you my number. I mean, I don't give my number to strangers on Facebook."

She hoped that he would understand and no be hurt by her message.

"So you think I am fake?"

Dianne tapped on her desk, thinking what to say next. "It's not that. We're just Facebook friends and let's keep it that way."

"I am a gentleman who knows how to treat a lady."

Dianne stared at the message for what seemed like hours, then finally typed in her number. After pressing the send button, she felt her heart beat nervously.

A few seconds later, her phone started to buzz. She picked it up nervously. She sighed with relief when she realized that it was just her best friend, Myah.

"Hey Dianne, I was thinking of checking out some clothes at Vision City and lunch after that. You wanna come?"

"Yes please."

"Cool! See you in a few minutes time."

"Dianne!" Myah exclaimed as she threw her arms around Dianne.

They embraced outside the Vision City mall. After they let go, they walked over to the entrance.

"So, where do you wanna go first?" Myah asked.

It was unusual for her to ask Dianne that because she would always pick the store and never gave Dianne a chance to pick.

"Well, maybe we should go to...."

"Oh!" Myah cut her off. "I know where we should go! Cherish!"

Dianne rolled her eyes as she followed Myah to the first floor of the mall where Cherish was located. It was an expensive clothing and jewelry shop. Dianne wasn't a huge fan of Cherish. She was more budget conscious and preferred the secondhand clothing shops.

While they were checking out the tops from the rack, Dianne's phone buzzed. She pulled it out of her pocket and a new number flashed on her screen. Her heart started pounding slowly. She walked away from Myah and answered the call.

"H-hello?"

"Hi!" an unfamiliar but friendly male voice said. "Is this Dianne?"

Her heart pounded faster. "Uhmm, y-yeah."

"Hi Dianne. This is William."

"Oh h-hi," she blurted.

"I was hoping we could catch up for lunch. Where are you?"

She pushed her hair back nervously. "Uh…I am at Vision City with my girlfriend at Cherish."

"Oh great! I am heading that way."

Dianne blushed and walked back to Cherish. She thought about William and her mind raced, not able to concentrate on what Myah was saying. It was wrong. She was a married woman. What if her husband Adam found out?

Some good twenty minutes later, her phone vibrated and she snapped out of her reverie. It was William!

"Hi, where are you?" she asked feeling excited.

"I'm outside Cherish. I got you and your friend Big Roster lunch packs and drinks."

Dianne paused for a moment. Wow! She would finally meet her cyber flirt William.

"Okay! We're coming out," she giggled. "Myah, let's go meet a friend. He's outside the shop."

Myah eyed her with a curious look. "Ok, who is he?"

Dianne started walking towards the door. "I'll fill you in with the details later. Come!"

Outside Cherish, a well-dressed man caught her eye. He wore an expensive suit. Dianne felt herself blush when he smiled at her. She felt her heart skip a few times.

He walked over to her. "Hi, are you Dianne?"

"Yes! You are William, right?"

He nodded. "Here's your Big Roster packs and drinks. And where's your friend?"

Dianne blushed. "She'll be here in a moment."

They started chatting about the weather and work. William seemed quite charming and Dianne could help but smile.

"Hi William!"

Myah cut into their conversation not sounding one bit happy. Dianne stood there flabbergasted. How on earth did Myah know William?

William's face went pale as if he'd seen a ghost. "Oh, hi Myah. I'll leave you two ladies. Got some stuff to complete at the office."

"Damn it Myah! Do you know William?" Dianne asked when he disappeared.

"Oh, he's a jerk! He's a womanizer that flirts with all the women on Facebook, picks them up with his maroon sports car, buys them lunch, sends them credits and all sorts of things to get into their pants."

Dianne frowned. "Oh shit!"

"Yeah, he has two kids from different women. He even messages women who have partners too. He kept sending me messages so Sam bashed him up at the Gold Club!"

"He asked to meet me to…"

"Stay away from that douchebag! He's a womanizer and sugar daddy!" Myah snapped. "You have a good husband and a handsome son."

Dianne bowed her head in defeat and embarrassment. She felt stupid to flip for William's sweet words on Facebook.

"Throw that crap away and let's go buy our own lunch," Myah said trying to lighten up Dianne's gloomy face.

"Thanks girl," she said sounding relieved.

Dianne dumped the Big Roster packs and drinks and they walked over to the Food Junction to buy lunch. She knew she could trust Myah. Both of them went way back to childhood. They shared secrets, confided with each other and watched each other's back.

How could she be so naïve and gullible? She pulled out her phone and quickly went onto Facebook and blocked William.

BUS RIDE

The bus stop in Down Town was crowded. It was about five o'clock in the afternoon and many of the office workers were rushing to get on the buses to go home. I worked as a junior accountant with the Price Waterhouse Coopers accounting firm that was located at Deloitte Tower. The roads in Down Town had been widened and traffic lights installed recently to cater for the ever increasing traffic.

I stood down the street from the traffic lights waiting to cross over to the bus stop. But seeing how quickly the vehicles were speeding by, and knowing how dangerous it was, I decided to walk up to the traffic lights and wait for them to change to red so I could cross.

An old man, one of the many beggars in town, sat beside the road with his arms outstretched. I felt sorry for him and dropped several one kina coins into the carton placed in front of him. I reached the traffic light area and waited with a group of people. Vehicles sped by sending their obnoxious fumes towards us. After some minutes, the traffic light changed to red and vehicles screeched to a halt behind the white lines - except for one vehicle that dashed through, just missing several people who'd started to cross the street.

Several people swore at the driver. Commuters in Port Moresby were too seasoned to trust the traffic lights completely.

"Asshole driver!" Someone shouted loudly at the driver.

"Seriously, that type of behaviour is why we never develop," I muttered.

I crossed briskly to the other side and other people crossed over to our previous side. There were two kai-bars and the smell emanating from those kai-bars tingled my nose. The mixture of garlic, lamb, fish and spices made a potent combination. I held my breath for a moment as I walked past feeling the pangs of hunger crawl up in my tummy. I always wondered how the people working inside the kai-bars could stand the smell. Perhaps they were used to it.

I made my way quickly towards the bus stop where there were so many people pushing and shoving to get on the buses. I stood patiently at the side, not wanting to be in the middle of the crowd. It was common for pickpockets to mingle with the crowd and when they rushed for a bus, the pickpockets would snatch commuters' *bilums* and bags. I carefully scanned the crowd for any police presence before going over to a highlands man who was standing nearby.

"*Buai stap ah?*" I asked.

"*Em stap. Wan kina lo wanpla,*" he quickly replied.

I handed him a two kina note. "*Tupla kam. Kambang wantaim.*"

He put his hand into a *bilum* hidden under his shirt and pulled out two betel nuts with mustard and a lime bottle. *Buai* sellers were very discreet with their business activities since the National Capital District Governor announced a ban on betel nut selling and chewing in Port Moresby city. I chewed the betel nut quickly and bought two cigarettes to smoke. The cigarettes made me feel relaxed from the stress at work.

After some time, the crowd lessened and several buses had some seats available. I boarded one of the buses. It was filled in no time with some passengers literally hanging onto the door of the bus. I secured a seat beside the window. An attractive young, working-class lady sat next to me. From her features, I guessed she was from Manus.

Putting on my headphones firmly on my ears, I watched the ocean as we passed Ela Beach on our way towards Koki Market. The afternoon breeze blew straight into my face and I thought back to my village where I would often go down to the beach and watch the beautiful sunset.

The pretty Manus lady tapped me on my arm and broke into my reverie. "Hey, the bus crew is collecting bus fares."

"Oh, okay."

I took out a one kina coin from my shirt pocket and handed it over to her to pass onto the bus crew.

At Koki Market, several passengers left and new ones got on. The bus sped off again towards Badili. There, some passengers got off. A group of men with eyes that clearly looked stoned from marijuana got on. One of them studied the passengers and said something to his friend.

The bus slowly climbed up Two Mile hill and one of the men from the group that had got on at Badili shouted for the driver to stop. The driver pulled up into the bus stop and, almost simultaneously, the men removed sharp, pointed knives from their pockets and the driver, bus crew and passengers were caught by surprise. The bus crew had a sharp knife against his throat.

"Hand over all your bags, mobile phones and wallets!" one of the men yelled at the passengers.

Everyone started handing over their possessions. The smallest of the group of men, who looked like he was from Goilala, walked over and tried to pull the bag off the Manus lady sitting next to me.

"Please...please don't take my bag..." she begged.

"Give me the damn bag or else..." he threatened her.

His breath smelled of alcohol and many of his teeth were rotting. The Manus lady kept holding onto her bag and I could tell that the small Goilala man was getting impatient. He suddenly stabbed her in the arm and she screamed in pain. The other women in the bus started screaming loudly in fear and the robbers panicked. I was scared and sat very still, hoping to prevent more bloodshed. Until that moment, I had never known the meaning of fear.

The Goilala man quickly snatched the Manus lady's bag and left the bus. His friends followed and they all ran down the hill towards the two-mile settlement. The Manus lady was bleeding badly and she was crying in pain. I used her face towel to apply some pressure to slow the bleeding.

I looked over to the driver. "Can we take her to the hospital please?"

"Yes, we'll go there then go over to Boroko."

We sped off towards the Port Moresby General Hospital. I turned back to the lady and asked for her name and if she wanted any of her family members to know about her condition. Luckily for me, the robbers didn't get to me and I still had my phone.

"My name is Angela. Please call my mum," she told me her mum's number.

I called Angela's mum and told her about her daughter and that she would be dropped off at the hospital.

After hanging up, I studied Angela. "You'll be okay on your own before your parents arrive?"

She kept sobbing and her eyes were filled with tears. "Can you stay with me please?"

I was starving and couldn't wait to get home and have dinner. But the poor lady looked so helpless and I couldn't leave her.

When we arrived at the hospital, I helped her out of the bus and to the emergency area. There was a long queue of patients and people there.

I started up a conversation with Angela, asking where she lived and worked. She answered all of my questions, keeping up the casual conversation and never taking her eyes off me.

It was going to be a long night ahead. I sighed, feeling hungry.

A week later after the incident on the bus, I was busy working on a client's tax returns when my mobile phone rang. It was a new number. I didn't like entertaining unknown numbers so decided to let in ring out. Some people didn't check their numbers properly and dialed the wrong numbers.

My phone kept ringing and I got really annoyed. "Yes! Who is this?"

"Hi," a female voice said. "Is this Tony?"

"Yes, and you are?"

"Hi Tony. It's me, Angela from the bus incident."

I remembered giving her my mobile number when she asked at the hospital. I calmed down.

"Hi Angela. How are you and how's your arm?"

"Still sore but I am okay. Hey, you want to hang out for lunch with me? My treat."

"Okay? I mean, sure."

"That's if you're single."

"What?" I was caught off guard with that remark.

"You scared? I don't bite."

"See you at lunch time then."

It was an adventurous bus ride after all, I thought and smiled at my computer like an idiot.

RASCAL IN PARADISE

Alfie couldn't bear the oppressive heat from the midday sun. He checked that the M16 assault rifle was hidden properly underneath his jacket and leaned against the street light pole pretending that he was resting. His eyes were red and he felt a little light headed from the marijuana joint he had smoked earlier.

From his vantage point outside he could see into the glass walls of the bank and watched the people inside doing their banking. Alfie studied the two security guards at the bank entrance. They were unarmed, but had a German Shepherd dog with them.

Three of his friends; Pitz, Buro and Wilz sat in a dark glassed Toyota Hilux vehicle parked a few metres away from him, all armed and waiting patiently for the right moment. One of the tellers, Joe, who lived at the same street at Morata had informed them that there would be a payroll run by the Oil Search company today. Oil Search usually withdrew over two hundred thousand kina in hard cash to pay for its casuals and laborers at their drilling sites in the jungles.

The bank robbery was a means to an end for Alfie. He grew up in the notorious squatter settlements of Morata. Life was a daily struggle for his family. He had completed grade twelve at Tokarara Secondary School two years ago and had been selected to attend the University of Papua New Guinea. But his parents couldn't afford the tuition fees. His father was unemployed and spent his days under the trees gambling and playing cards with the other men from the settlement. His mother would harvest *kango* from the nearby swamp and sell it at the market every day. The little money she made would be used for food. However, she had been recently diagnosed with a brain tumor and needed money to go for further treatment in Australia. His share of the money from the robbery would be used to support his impoverished family and pay for his mother's medical bills.

Alfie remembered when she had had a fit. They took her immediately to the hospital. She could barely keep her eyes open and was admitted to the emergency ward. The doctor announced that she had cancer in the brain and needed chemotherapy treatment which was not available in Papua New Guinea.

"She needs immediate help, but it won't be cheap. She needs to go to Australia for an operation," the doctor had said. "I hope you find the money."

So weeks had passed and every day Alfie would go visit his mother. He told her that he was going to find a way to get the thirty thousand kina that was needed for her treatment. Now was his only chance to get that money.

Alfie felt nervous. So many *rascals* had been killed by the police. He rubbed the sweat on his face, trying to focus on the plan. They had planned to hold the Oil Search pick-up vehicle at gun point as soon as the cash was withdrawn and brought out of the bank. Alfie's job was to make sure no one came near the vicinity of the bank when the robbery was taking place.

An Oil Search company vehicle pulled up next to the Hilux at exactly one o'clock, just as Joe had mentioned. A blue police vehicle with two policemen escorted it. A smartly dressed employee of Oil Search walked into the bank and, after some minutes, walked out with a large trunk box. The security guards assisted him to carry it to the waiting company vehicle. It was time to move!

The doors of the Hilux opened. Pitz jumped out and fired a volley of shots at the policemen. Both of them fell down instantly. Buro jumped out from the other side and shot the dog before yelling at the security guards and the Oil Search employee carrying the trunk box to lie face down on the pavement.

Alfie quickly slipped a black mask over his head and pulled out the M16 rifle. His hands were shaking and thinking normally he would have reconsidered his options. But he was drugged and his body was full of adrenaline. He cocked the rifle and ran over to the middle of the road.

"Down on the ground! Nobody move or I'll blow your brains off!" Alfie yelled and pointed the rifle at the crowd of by standers. They scattered in fear.

"Put the trunk box onto the Hilux now!" Pitz ordered the guards.

They complied submissively and loaded the trunk box on the getaway vehicle. Pitz kept the gun pointed at the guards. "On the ground, now!"

Pitz then signaled the boys to retreat back to the Hilux. Wilz had the engine running and he rammed it several times, ready for a fast take off. Alfie gave a warning shot before running over to the Hilux and jumped in quickly. Wilz reversed and quickly accelerated down the road towards the freeway. They overtook several vehicles before turning off into the road leading towards the airport and the Hiritano Highway.

Police vehicles were nowhere to be seen. Alfie felt a sense of relief run through his shaking body. They needed to get to nine mile and take the back road to Gerehu Stage Seven fast. At this point, every police vehicle in the city would be on alert. Pitz quickly cut open the locks on the trunk box and loaded all the hundred and fifty kina notes into an old bag they had brought. It wasn't long before they reached the outskirts of Gerehu Stage Seven via the back road. No one was in sight. They quickly changed into different clothes and abandoned the Hilux. They had loaded their guns into hiking bags and separated to catch PMV buses without raising any sort of alarm. They all made it back to Morata safely. Their plan had worked out perfectly. Or so Alfie thought.

It was late in the evening and Alfie wanted to drink beer. His mouth watered at the prospect of a cold carton of South Pacific lager. That afternoon they had distributed the cash among themselves, including Joe, and he was given forty thousand kina as his share. Alfie had never had such a large amount of money in his whole life. He gave thirty nine thousand kina to his mother for her medical bills as well as to buy food for the house. The remaining one thousand kina was his to burn.

Alfie found Pitz at the buai market. Pitz was drunk and chatting away with the buai sellers. Pitz took a SP bottle out of his pocket and offered him.

Pitz was in a merry mood. "Cheers brother! Drink!"

Alfie opened the bottle with his teeth and took a large gulp of the beer quenching his thirst. It tasted really good.

He tossed his bottle against Pitz's bottle. "Ah-h, this is real beer. Cheers!"

He removed a hundred kind from his pocket and sent a boy to buy a carton of beer from the nearby trade store. By the sixth bottle, Alfie was drunk. The sort of drunken state where everything is beautiful and perfect and every woman looks like an angel. A woman walked by and he whistled at her but she ignored him.

"Naispla ya! Nogat makmak na moson!"

"She's married bro," Pitz commented.

"Who gives a shit brother!"

Alfie and Pitz finished drinking the carton of beer and walked over to the trade store and bought another carton.

"Let's go to your house and drink there," Pitz suggested.

Alfie was already really drunk. "Ok, let's go."

"Carry the carton and go first. I'll look for Wilz and Buro and we'll come over to your place."

As he passed the side street leading to his house, Alfie heard someone tell him to stand still. He turned ninety degrees to face the voice. The empty street was littered with semi-permanent houses and insufficiently lit by sickly yellow street lights. Alfie was drunk and seeing double figures so he couldn't work out who they were.

"Who are you?"

"Stand where you are! Don't move!" one of them ordered.

He was older and clearly a person of authority. The other two young policemen stood on either side of him. The older policeman looked overweight but he pulled a pistol from his side and pulled the hammer. Click.

Oh shit! Police! Alfie realized. But it was too late.

If he ran, he'd be shot in the back. The prospect of being shot in the back was not something he relished.

"Where did you get the money to drink?"

Alfie tried to sober up and act normal. "Ah-h boss, it's from my market money."

"You're under arrest."

The policemen surrounded him. Two of them hauled him towards the police vehicle that was parked in the dark with its lights turned off. Alfie tried to protest but felt a fist land on his jaw. He fell on the ground letting go of the beer carton. Several bottles smashed when the carton landed on the ground.

The next thing Alfie knew, he was on the ground trying to protect himself from three sets of boots. They were all around him. He writhed on the ground. Alfie raised his arms trying in vain to fend off the next attack.

"Boss, please I didn't do anything," he cried.

Alfie tried to shield himself, tried to find some sanctuary from the blows. It felt as though pain was a volume switch being turned up and up in different parts of his body. He rolled over on his back just in time to see the butt of a gun.

Everything went black.

Some hours later, Alfie opened his eyes slowly. A white light from the ceiling dazed him. He was unsure whether it was because of the brightness of the light or if it was because he was unadjusted to the light. After squinting a little, his vision cleared up and he saw a brick wall and iron bars blocking off any possibility of escape. He was in a prison. It took him a minute to figure out what the hell he would be doing in a prison.

All of a sudden he had a flashback. Alfie remembered the three policemen kicking the living daylights out of him. At exactly the same time he felt the pain. It ran through the length of his body. He couldn't feel his arms or legs or his chest, only the pain. Alfie closed his eyes trying to forget the pain. The thought of his mother receiving first class medical treatment in Australia made him smile for a while. He loved her very much.

AFTERNOON ENCOUNTER

It was a just another usual fortnight Friday afternoon. The clock in my office showed four-thirty pm. I saved the cashbook and ledgers I was working on and shut down my laptop, feeling happy that the weekend had finally arrived. It was a stressful week sorting out payments and allowances for the provincial health officers to do their routine supervisory visits to the districts.

I was about twenty four years old and a contract staff of an Australian Aid development program based at the Milne Bay Provincial Health Office in Alotau. I managed the Health Sector Improvement Program Trust Account and all donor funds given for health programs in the province. It was a demanding job but I was an enthusiastic and smart young accountant who managed the trust account prudently. My bosses were proud of me. Even the staff at the National Department of Health spoke highly of me. In fact, Milne Bay province was ranked as the top-performing province in terms to key health indicators partly due to my contribution.

The afternoon sun was still burning hot when I walked out of the office. My boss was also leaving the office. "You have a nice weekend."

"Thanks boss," I replied and watched him drive off in the fifth element vehicle that had been purchased from the trust account.

One day I'll be a boss too, I thought and sighed.

I stood for a while under the tree beside the office to shelter from the heat thinking of what to do or where to go next. Pulling out my cellphone, I found Brendan's number and called him.

Brendan was my schoolmate and friend from Cameron Secondary School. He had dropped out of grade ten while I continued to grade eleven and twelve, then onto university. But he managed to get into a family business and was doing quite well. He had a Toyota Corolla, which he allowed me to use from time to time for urgent runs, go out partying or to take ladies out on a date. I dated a new lady almost every month. I didn't know whether it was my good looks or the money, but I didn't care. I was only concerned about getting laid. Brendan jokingly called me 'Elvis Priestley' because of my prowess with the ladies.

"Yes Elvis," Brendan answered.

"Bro, you have any bright plans for tonight?"

"Nothing interesting. What are you up to?"

"Just want to have a few drinks and watch karaoke at Airways."

"Cool, so where are you now?"

Brendan loved drinking beer and it showed on his protruding tummy. He was a slim guy but had put on a few kilograms lately due to his alcohol consumption.

"I am outside my office but will walk over to the beachfront market to look for *buai* and cigarettes while waiting for you," I said

"Okay, give me thirty minutes to sort out a few things."

It was almost five o'clock and the sun was losing its heat now. I walked slowly over to the market at the Sanderson Bay beachfront. It was only a three minutes stroll away from my office.

The beachfront was a hive of activity and people. The pathway from one end of the bay to the other was littered on both sides with street vendors with their tables and umbrellas. I would sometimes joke and call this area, the 'Umbrella City' of Alotau. People from the surrounding squatter settlements and the cargo boats at dock would mingle around here until late at night. The informal street market flourished and the vendors would make about four to five hundred kina a day selling their items there. They sold items from scones, betel nuts, cigarettes and cordial drinks to diving torches, sunglasses, clothes and fuel.

At around four pm when the main market in town closed, the villagers would bring their vegetables, fish, fruits, and other garden food that were not bought to the Sanderson Bay beachfront to sell and make extra money before boarding the late PMVs at six pm to head back to their villages along the highway to East Cape and Garuahi on the north coast.

The first vendor's table from my office, near the small creek from Duau Compound was my favorite table. Bolo, the young man that manned it was from Suau and had become my good friend after realizing that I was a frequent customer to his table. For me, it was the convenience of not having to walk further to buy a cigarette. He would allow me to collect cigarettes and *buai* on credit when I was short on cash and when my pay came in on business week, I would pay for it. I always paid up and he trusted me.

"Afternoon boss," Bolo greeted me.

"Good afternoon. Looks like a busy afternoon," I said observing the place.

He smiled. "You know it already."

I knew from the smile that he had made a fair amount of money today. I've had several friendly chats on my frequent visits for cigarettes with Bolo about his informal business and his aspirations. Bolo was a grade eight dropout from the village school and had come to town to live with his uncle at the settlement on the hillside. His uncle had given him one hundred kina to buy a few items to sell and now he had saved over a thousand kina in his Micro-Finance Bank account. Bolo wanted to make enough money to buy a dinghy and outboard motor to go fishing and then sell his catch at the market. I admired his determination.

The sun was slowing disappearing over the Pini Range at the western end of the bay. Bolo handed me a stool from his market table to sit down. I watched the working class people with vehicles parked beside the road and hurried about to grab some vegetables for dinner. I checked the time on my cell phone. It was only five twenty pm. There was still time before Brendan arrived.

I grabbed a *buai* from Bolo's table and husked it before chewing it with mustard and lime. Then got five cigarettes. *Buai* goes well with cigarettes and I felt good. I gave Bolo a fifty kina note and collected twenty kina worth of flex cards. Bolo calculated the amount for the flex cards, cigarettes and betel nuts before giving my change.

I gave him a five kina note. "Go buy yourself a drink."

He smiled in appreciation. "Thanks boss!"

I quickly entered the flex card numbers and subscribed for a data package from Digicel to access my Facebook account. I was pretty addicted to Facebook and would spend a lot of money buying flex cards. My mum would advise me to cut down on the flex, but what the heck! It was my money and I made my own decisions.

Then, I saw him!

An old man in his late fifties who probably lived in one of the nearby squatter settlements. He wore an old shirt and had some white hair. What caught my attention was that he kept looking at a bunch of bananas on sale. He turned it over and over, felt it, asked how much it was then walked away quietly. Some minutes later, he walked back again and asked the lady who was selling the bananas again. She told him the price and the old man walked away again.

I kept watching the old man intrigued by his movements. He stood under the nearby tree deep in thought for probably fifteen minutes and then walked back to the lady selling the bananas. Again, she told him the price. He bowed his head in defeat and walked away.

Something bothered me so I stopped him when he passed by Bolo's table on his way to Duau Compound, the squatter settlement nearby.

"Hey, father, you okay?" I asked.

The old man didn't reply. He just looked at me. He looked worried and helpless. I could see the pain in his eyes.

"I saw you going back and forth checking the bunch of bananas over there," I said trying to get him to talk.

"I can't afford them. She couldn't reduce the price. It's four kina and I have only two kina," he muttered and bowed his head.

"What were you planning on doing with them?"

"I have nothing at home. Those bananas would make my family a good meal. Maybe one banana each, but still okay."

His response broke my heart! I couldn't utter a single word and suddenly felt a pain inside me for the old man and his family.

Here I was spending so much money on unnecessary things while a fellow countryman had only two kina in his pocket and a family to feed!

I felt my entire body tremble with guilt. My conscience was bothered. I pulled out a fifty kina note from my wallet and gave it to him. "Here, go buy the banana and some protein for your dinner."

He stood there completely lost not knowing what to do, whether to smile or cry. After a moment's silence, he looked at me. This time I saw a bright look in his eyes.

"Thank you very much, son. I don't know how I can repay your kindness but God will surely bless you," he said with tears in his eye.

"Don't worry about it father. Just go buy the banana before the lady hops on the next PMV."

"Okay, but thank you again. God bless your kind heart," he said before walking back to the lady selling the banana.

"You're welcome."

I felt his words and slowly took in a deep breath.

Deep inside, I felt that I had done something good. I had helped a man in need.

Brendan arrived some time later looking excited. He had parked the Corolla on the other side of the market and walked over to Bolo's table. He knew that was my favorite table and would find me there.

"Have a cigarette and chew one *buai* bro," I said when he arrived.

He got two cigarettes and lit one. "Thanks bro. So what's the plan? We go grab a six pack from Toto's black market to warm up before going to Airways?"

"Nah, I changed my mind bro. I'll give you some money to get your six-pack. I don't feel like going out."

"What?"

Brendan looked at me in disbelief.

"Yup, drop me off at home. I'll give you fifty kina for your six pack."

"Okay Elvis. Something happened?"

I told him about the encounter with the old man and Brendan finally understood.

"I think you're right. Get us some *buai* and cigarettes and I'll drop you off at home. We can go out another time."

"Thanks bro," I said feeling relieved.

We bought about twenty kina worth of betel nuts and a packet of cigarettes from Bolo before leaving for Brendan's vehicle.

The sun had gone and darkness was crawling in. My mind wandered off to the families all over the country who would be cooking their meals at this time. Some would be cooking delicious meals with chicken or lamb or fish. Others would be dining at expensive hotels. Others would make do with whatever little they had and others may go to bed hungry and hoping that the next day would turn out better. The old man would cook the bunch of bananas. I hoped he had bought some *aibika* and fish to go with the bananas.

THE LOST PUPPY

My mother gave birth to five puppies. I was the fifth. My mother named me Snoopy and took care of me just like the other puppies. I was small and fluffy with big brown eyes. I had white fur with a few black spots.

The people who took care of us wanted to sell me to a new owner because there were too many of us. My mother tried to protect me from being taken away, growling and barking angrily at them but they hit her with a stick and loaded me into a car. I was only a few months old.

Anyway, my new owner took me to his house. Everything looked strange to me and I started missing my mother. I climbed out of my box and looked around. Everyone was busy watching television. I walked out of the door quietly and went to a nearby tree to pee.

"Hey you!" a big dog shouted angrily. "That's my peeing spot!"

I ran for my life. The big dog now had his gang chasing me. I ran across the busy road and they immediately stopped.

A car went by, nearly hitting me. I ducked as another car went by. Then, a bus nearly crushed me but the person controlling the bus swerved at the last second and nearly crashed into the dogs. I ran off down the street not knowing where I was going.

That night, I felt lonely and howled while looking at the moon wondering how the other puppies were doing. I curled up into a ball and fell asleep.

The sun was up and I went to a nearby restaurant where they threw food scraps and bones at me because of pity or something. I saw someone check out a page of the newspaper about RSPCA. It was the home for stray dogs.

I immediately set off to find the place. I came across some signposts pointing in different directions and was confused. Then I saw another fellow dog.

"Hi buddy!" I shouted. "Can you help me find the RSPCA?"

"What's that?" he asked curiously.

I explained to him what it was and he showed me the right direction.

"Wait!" he exclaimed as I was about to leave. "Maybe I could come too..."

"Sure buddy," I said.

With my new friend, we searched for the RSPCA all over the city. One night, I was sleeping in an alley. My buddy was looking for food. All of a sudden, I was woken up by fierce barking. It was that big dog and his gang.

"You nearly got all of us killed!" he shrieked. "Now, I'm going to return the favor."

My buddy saw what was happening and launched himself at the big dog. A big fight broke out and I was been cornered by the big dog's gang. They launched at me and I ran out to the road without thinking.

Wham! I got hit by a car and fell unconscious.

I woke up some hours later in the RSPCA and saw a little boy looking at me. "Mummy, I want that puppy."

JORDAN DEAN

THE GHOST

At half past six, I completed the payroll input and walked out of my office. A heavy downpour began as I made my way quickly to the bus stop outside Port Moresby General Hospital. My black suit and extension hair were soaked by the time I got to the empty bus stop.

I felt like a soaked, ugly duckling and spent a few minutes trying to fix my hair. I didn't expect the heavy rain that evening so I wasn't able to bring an umbrella. Half of my body was wet and I wanted to get home as soon as possible.

Just then, a taxi came down the road and I waved frantically at the driver. He pulled over and stopped beside me.

"Good evening. Gerehu please."

The taxi driver unlocked the doors and I jumped into the backseat. He was a middle aged, highlands man. Apart from the unshaven beard, he looked quite friendly. We headed towards Waigani.

The hazy windscreen reflected a blaze of colour. Red car tail lights, orange street lights, and white headlights of the oncoming vehicles. The traffic was horrendous when we got to the central Waigani area.

I snuggled myself to keep warm but the air condition made me shiver. "Bestie, turn off the air condition please. I am cold!"

"Kaiye, mi hot eh na yu kol ah?"

"Yeah. I was freezing the whole day. Now, turn off the air condition or I'll catch another taxi."

He studied me in the rear view mirror. "Eeh, yu tok eh. Yu stap lo wanem hap na yu kol?"

"Geez! I was at the hospital!"

His jaw literally dropped. "Kaiye, mi nonap go lo Gerehu. Yu go daun na kalap lo nadla taxi."

"What? Stop the vehicle then. I'll get another taxi!" I snapped, checking the time on my phone. "Damn it! It's getting late!"

"Bestie eh, yu stap lo wanem hap lo em kol na yu tok?"

The taxi driver rubbed his forehead, looking confused. He started to get on my nerves with his endless questions.

"Wiesssh, stop the bloody vehicle now!"

"Kaiye bestie eh, plis yu tok gut pastaim. Yu stap lo wanem hap na yu kam? Nogut yu stap lo morgue na kam."

I thought he was joking but realised he had beads of sweat on his forehead. I could see the fear in his eyes. "So you thought I was a ghost?"

"Aiyo, plis yu tok stret ya!" he pleaded.

"Sorry bestie. I meant that I was in an air conditioned office all day. Then I got soaked in the rain and your taxi's air condition is making me really cold. I work at the hospital. What makes you think I am a ghost?"

He looked back at me nervously. "Yu wearim black black na gras blo yu luk nadla kain. Olsem na mi ting yu tewel eh."

His facial expression got me in stitches. "Bestie, I am not a ghost. I am human like you."

He sighed, finally relieved that I wasn't a ghost. "Yu tu ya bestie. Mekim na skin gras blo mi sanap natin. Okay, yumi go na mi lusim yu lo haus door blo yu."

I couldn't stop myself from laughing the entire ride home.

ILLEGAL LOGGING

It was a sunny afternoon. I was heading home, exhausted from a stressful day at work. As I was walked up towards the overhead bridge next to the main entrance of the Vision City shopping mall, there was a commotion right at the landing of the stairway. Like everybody else, I rushed to see what the commotion was about.

There were two women grabbing each other's neck and hailing obscene, derogatory words of the female genitalia among others, mixed in with Tok Pisin and a local dialect of a highlands region. One was a middle aged woman, probably in her mid-forties, and the other was a teenager.

The oncoming traffic slowed down to get a glimpse of the commotion too. There was a loose circle of laughing men following the tassel who seemed to be enjoying the show. Among them were the security personnel, guarding the gate with their white and black uniforms. Several women passing by to catch a bus on the other side of the overhead bridge giggled, holding their hands over their mouths to conceal their laughter. A crowd gathered along the bridge, looking down just like in a sporting arena observing with intense interest.

I walked over to one of the guards. "Hey, yupla stopim ol! Yupla mekim wanem na lukluk tasol? Stopim ol nau. Nogut ol bai kilim ol yet lo hia."

Someone echoed the same concerned sentiments and their security training kicked in. They held the two women and dragged them apart. The younger woman walked away towards the bus stop while the older woman kept snarling with her *meri blouse* half torn.

"Ol koros lo illegal logging ya!"

One *buai* seller said, and a cracking laughter echoed. A few sarcastic comments came from the lively crowd that started to disperse. Then, everything went back to normal as if nothing happened. I looked at the *buai* seller confused. What did he mean by 'illegal logging'?

Still bothered by the expression and not wanting to be left in the dark with the latest street slang, I approached the *buai* seller.

"Bestie, wanpla buai kam," I said, handing him one kina. "Illegal logging em wanem?"

"Ah, em olsem taim narapla meri stealim diwai blo narapla. Bigpla problem ya."

His analogy and facial expression cracked me up. "Tru ya bestie! Ol mas fait lo diwai tasol."